In memory of my Dad ~ C F

For Isaac and Daniel ~ J C

Copyright © 2009 by Good Books, Intercourse, PA 17534
International Standard Book Number: 978-1-56148-658-8

Library of Congress Catalog Card Number: 2008029260

Text copyright © Claire Freedman 2009
Illustrations copyright © Jane Chapman 2009
Original edition published in English by Little Tiger Press,
an imprint of Magi Publications, London, England, 2009.

Printed in China
Library of Congress Cataloging-in-Publication Data
Freedman, Claire.
When we're together / Claire Freedman ; [illustrated by] Jane Chapman.
p. cm.
Summary: Rhyming text celebrates the simple pleasures of time spent together with family or friends.
ISBN 978-1-56148-658-8 (hardcover : alk. paper)
[1. Stories in rhyme. 2. Friendship--Fiction. 3. Family life--Fiction.] I. Chapman, Jane, 1970- ill.
II. Title. III. Title: When we are together.
PZ8.3.F88Wh 2009
[E]--dc22
2008029260

When We're Together

Claire Freedman   Jane Chapman

Good Books®

Intercourse, PA 17534
800/762-7171
www.GoodBooks.com

Together is waking to bright summer sunshine,
With happy songs filling your head,
It's singing the words at the top of your voice
As you bounce up and down on your bed.

Being together is running down hillsides,
So fast that you almost can't stop!
Together is landing in one giant heap,
And catching your breath as you flop.

Together's the fun that you have when it's snowing,
The sleighs that you can't wait to ride,
It's giggling while trying to hold up each other
Whenever your feet slip and slide!

Being together is having a secret
To share with your very best friends,
It's talking and listening and laughing together,
And knowing your friendship won't end.

Time spent together is getting all messy,
It's squidgy mud pies that you pat,
It's squashing and squelching
and stamping them down,
And hearing the sound as they splat!

Together is riding on Daddy's
strong shoulders,
And feeling as tall as a tree,
It's going exploring and having adventures,
And sharing new things that you see.

Together is kicking through leaves,
crisp and crunchy,
And watching them swirl through the air,
It's leaping in piles that come up to your knees,
And showering the leaves everywhere.

Being together is fireside snuggles,
It's magical stories you share,
It's hearing the rain pitter-pat on the windows,
While squished in your favorite chair.

Together is searching in seaweedy rock pools,
Then catching a crab in your hand,
It's squealing as waves rush over your feet,
And wiggling your toes in the sand.

Sometimes together is just being quiet,
And gazing at clouds in the sky,
It's seeing the shapes and the patterns they make,
And counting them as they float by.

Together is pillow fights all 'round your bedroom,
And giggling and running to hide,
It's white fluffy feathers that fly through the air
So it looks like it's snowing inside.

Time spent together is big hugs at bedtime,
And being tucked in snug and tight,
It's sweet dreams and moonbeams
and drowsy eyes closing,
And sleeping safe all through the night.